First published in Great Britain by Pelham Books Ltd,
27 Wrights Lane, London W8 5TZ in 1987

First published in Denmark by Gyldendalske Boghandel
as *Lavinen kommer* in 1986

British Library Cataloguing in Publication Data

Svend, Otto S.
  Avalanche!
  I. Title II. Lavinen Kommer. *English*
  839.8′1374[J]   PZ7
   ISBN 0-7207-1732-9

Printed in Denmark

SVEND OTTO S

Avalanche!

Translated by Joan Tate

PELHAM BOOKS

Carl lived on a farm in a valley below the mountains. Usually, there was thick snow on the ground all winter.

This January, his friend Martin was coming for a skiing holiday. But the snow was hard and slippery – good for the sledge, but hopeless for skiing.

Martin arrived, and with him came the new snow.

For three days, the blizzard raged. They just managed to keep the path between the house and the barn clear, but could hardly see more than a few feet in front of them. The snow was much too deep and soft for skiing.

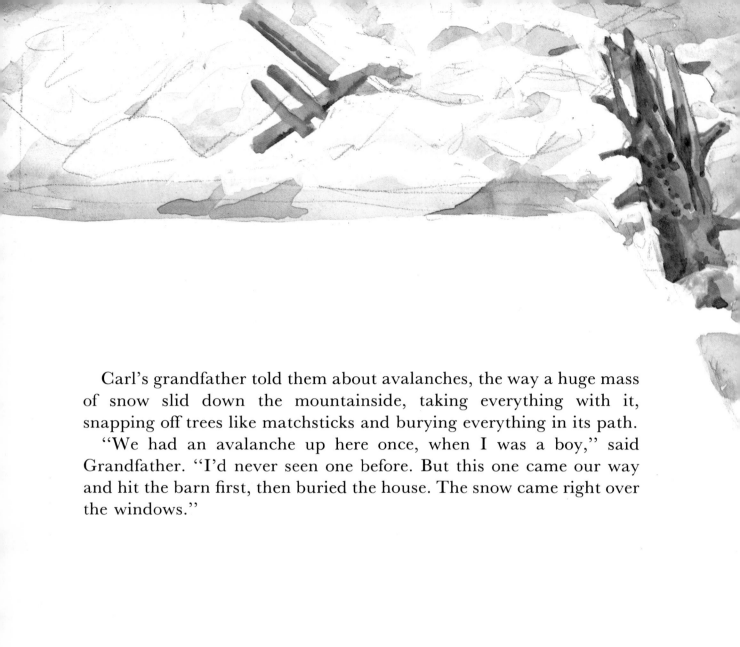

Carl's grandfather told them about avalanches, the way a huge mass of snow slid down the mountainside, taking everything with it, snapping off trees like matchsticks and burying everything in its path.

"We had an avalanche up here once, when I was a boy," said Grandfather. "I'd never seen one before. But this one came our way and hit the barn first, then buried the house. The snow came right over the windows."

"How did you get out?" said Martin.

"First we had to let the fire out and wait for the chimney to cool," said Grandfather. "Then I had to crawl up the chimney and on to the roof. I was the smallest, you see. And I looked like a chimney-sweep, too, when I got out!"

"The first thing I did was to look for my dog. I was afraid he'd been buried, like the sheep. But he hadn't. He was trapped in a space under the eaves when the barn collapsed. He wasn't hurt at all. I was as pleased to see him as he was to see me."

"I've never seen an avalanche," said Martin. "What should you do?"

"You should keep away from steep slopes," said Grandfather. "But if you do see one coming, get rid of your skis and ski-sticks. They drag you down. Then curl up with your arms in front of your face, so you've got some air."

"I think we'll just keep out of the way," said Carl.

Next day, the weather cleared and the sun came out. The snow sparkled like diamonds and was fine for skiing as they set out.

Every day, Martin and Carl went skiing as far as they could go up the side of the valley. When the sun began to sink below the mountains, they turned back and sped downhill all the way home, the snow flying up all round them.

On the last day of Martin's holiday, the weather began to break. It was still fine, but the wind had got up and great grey clouds were beginning to drift over the mountain peaks. So they turned and set off home.

Carl suddenly stopped and pointed.

"Look!" he cried. "Those two men right up there – they must be crazy. They're coming down one of the worst places! Look, Martin!"

As he spoke, there was a tremendous roaring sound and it looked as if the whole mountain was moving. A huge mass of snow began to slide down, faster and faster, towards the two men.

One of the men seemed to be trying to get away to one side, but the snow was now racing down like an express train, and while the boys looked on, the two men disappeared completely.

Carl and Martin were knocked flat by the wave of air pressure.

"Let's get out of here!" shouted Martin over the noise.

"No, it's all right," Carl shouted back. "It won't go any further now."

He was right. The avalanche had stopped and was now a gigantic heap of huge chunks and blocks of snow.

"I must get back home and tell Dad to phone for help," said Carl. "You stay here and keep an eye on the place where they disappeared."

Carl skied away, leaving Martin on his own. It was quite quiet now, the only sound coming from small chunks of snow trickling and rolling down the slope.

Although it seemed a very long time to Martin, only about twenty minutes later he heard the sound of a helicopter clattering closer and closer.

As it came nearer, he waved and the helicopter landed in a huge swirl of snow.

Carl jumped out first and ran over to Martin.

"Have you seen anything?" he said.

"Nothing," said Martin.

"Here they come," said Carl, pointing at a line of men coming up the hillside towards them. "They were quick. Dad phoned at once."

"Who are they?" shouted Martin.

"The Mountain Rescue Team," said Carl. "Men from the village. The man in front is the leader. He's our policeman."

The men were all taking off their skis, and some were putting up a tent. The leader was directing them and placing look-outs to watch for any more landslips.

"Do you remember where the men disappeared?" he asked.
Martin nodded.
"Then you go in the helicopter and show the pilot."
The policeman turned to the other men and sent those with dogs further up with orders to let them rest on their mats. Then he led the way with his own dog, the other men behind him in a line.

In the helicopter, Martin looked down and saw the men fixing together thin steel rods as they moved up the hillside.

"What are they doing?" asked Martin.

"They're probing the snow," said the pilot. "The rods have rounded tips so as not to hurt anyone underneath. Was it here the first man disappeared?"

"No, further up," said Martin, pointing. It was hard to judge distances from above. "About there, I think."

"Then we'll mark it and fly on down. What about the second one?"

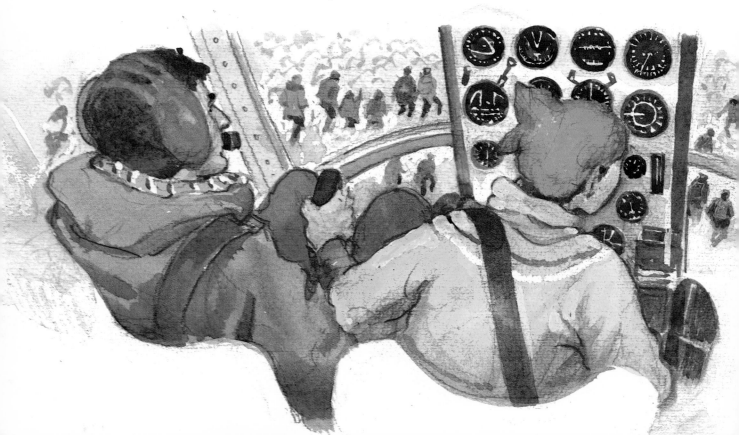

They flew back and forth over the great mass of snow below, looking for signs – for a glove, or a ski-stick, or a cap. Then they turned back and landed. Martin joined Carl and the other men, now shoulder to shoulder, prodding the snow with their rods.

The policeman was directing his own dog.

"Seek it out!" he shouted. "Seek!"

The dog clambered over the blocks of snow, sniffing and searching.

After ten minutes, the dog's sense of smell was paralysed by the cold. So another dog was brought up. The men went on prodding.

Suddenly a dog started scrabbling wildly in the snow. The men at once took their snow shovels from their backpacks and quickly started digging.

The dog grew more and more excited as they patted and praised it. Then a great shout went up.

"The sledge! Bring the sledge! We've found one!"

The unconscious man was strapped to the stretcher-sledge, while the others went on searching.

"Seek!" they kept shouting. "Seek it out!"

One dog after another had to be taken out of the search to rest, their paws bleeding from cuts made by the ice.

The policeman looked at his watch. "It'll soon be too late, even if he's still alive. He can't have much air left. And the dogs are getting very tired."

"Let's try that old trick," said one of the men. "Bury *me* in the snow."

That's just what they did. They buried him in the snow without the dog seeing. When the dog found him, they praised and patted it. So the dog was ready and eager to search again.

It raced off, then suddenly stopped and started digging.
"Shovels!" shouted the men.

They dug and dug and dug. Then a glove, and a red sleeve appeared.
They'd found him and he was still alive! The dog had felt the warmth of
his body through the snow.

After the injured man had been given first-aid in the tent, the helicopter flew him off to hospital.

Fifty exhausted men collected up their belongings and set off downhill, back to a hot meal and their ordinary jobs.

Martin, Carl and his father went back to the farm.

"I'll never forget that," said Martin. "Those men and dogs were amazing."

Carl's father looked up at the mountain.

"All went well this time," he said. "But it's not always like that. You never know what the mountain will do next. It can be quite a different story."